Dora and the Rainbow Kite Festival

by Christine Ricci illustrated by Robert Roper

Ready-to-Read

Simon Spotlight/Nick Jr.
New York London Toronto Sydney

Based on the TV series *Dora the Explorer®* as seen on Nick Jr.®

SIMON SPOTLIGHT
An imprint of Simon & Schuster Children's Publishing Division
1230 Avenue of the Americas, New York, New York 10020

Manufactured in the United States of America
10
Library of Congress Cataloging-in-Publication Data
Ricci, Christine.
Dora and the Rainbow Kite Festival / by Christine Ricci ; illustrated by Robert Roper.
—1st ed.
p. cm. — (Ready-to-read) (Dora the explorer)
"Based on the TV series Dora the Explorer as seen on Nick Jr."
ISBN-13: 978-1-4169-4777-6
ISBN-10: 1-4169-4777-9
0310 LAK
I. Roper, Robert. II. Dora the explorer (Television program)
III. Title.
PZ7.R355Dkr 2008
2006103142

Hi! I am DORA.

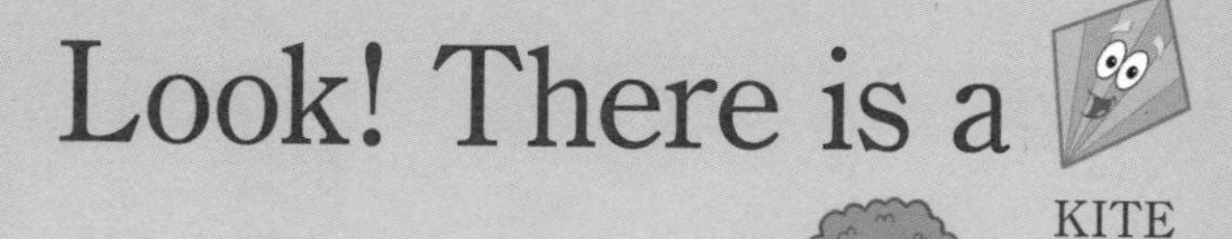

Look! There is a KITE

stuck in that TREE.

We have to help her!

How can we reach
the top of the TREE?
I have a ROPE in my BACKPACK.

We need the longest 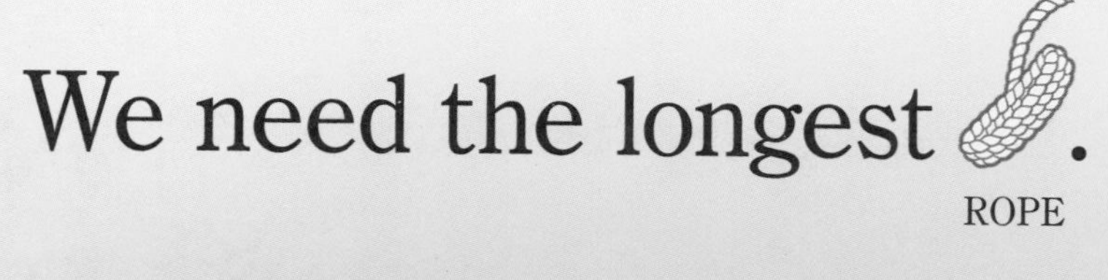.

Do you see it?

BOOTS is a great climber!

BOOTS rescued the KITE!

The has to get to
KITE
the Festival
RAINBOW KITE
before the disappears.
RAINBOW
Will you help us?

How do we get to

the RAINBOW KITE Festival?

Let's ask MAP!

MAP says the RAINBOW KITE Festival is at the top of Tallest MOUNTAIN.

First we go past the WINDMILL.

Then we go through RAINBOW DOOR.

We made it to the  .

WINDMILL

It is so windy!

We need to turn off the  WINDMILL

so the KITE can fly by.

But the WIND is blowing us

away from the SWITCH.

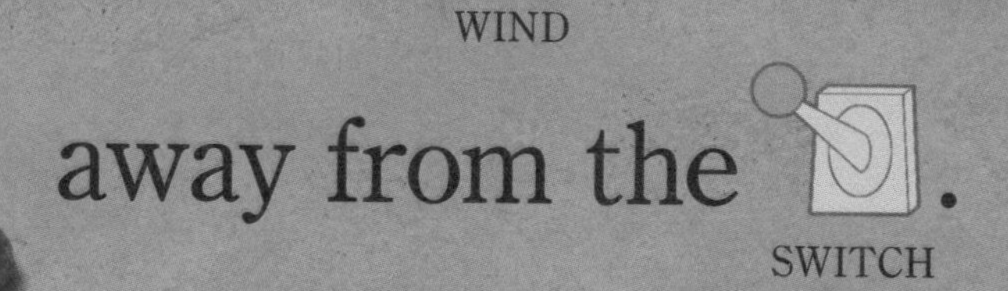

I know!

I need STRING to make a LASSO.

Do you see any STRING?

The little KITE has STRING!

We lassoed the  SWITCH

and stopped the  WIND!

RAINBOW DOOR has 7 LOCKS!
SEVEN

Can you find 7 KEYS
SEVEN

to match the 7 LOCKS?
SEVEN

Oh, no! I see SWIPER.

He will try to swipe the KEYS.

We have to stop him.

Say “SWIPER, no swiping!”

We stopped  !

The 7 keys opened the 7 locks on rainbow door.

Next comes Tallest 

.

There it is!

We have to hurry!

The RAINBOW is starting to fade!

Tallest

is so tall!

How can we get to the top?

The KITE can fly us
to the top of the MOUNTAIN.
We can hold on to her RIBBONS!

We made it to the

RAINBOW KITE Festival!

All of the 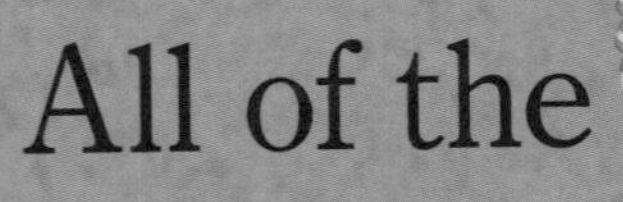 KITES are so happy.

But where is the  RAINBOW?

Say "Come back, RAINBOW!"

The  [RAINBOW] heard us

and came back.

Look at his colors!

The KITES are ready to fly.

Here they go!

Look at all of the  KITES

flying under the 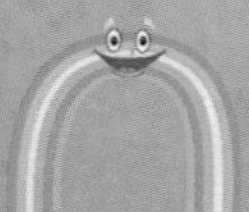 RAINBOW!

We did it!

Thanks for helping!